Dress-Up Princess Activity Book

Follow the instructions to dress up your princess. Try out your ideas on the style pages, then have fun creating beautiful, new outfits. There are also lots of fun princess activities to complete!

make believe ideas

1

Lay the board on a flat surface and then choose some fabric from the pack.

2

Lift the top of the board and begin by laying the fabric on the princess until she is completely covered.

3

Close the top of the board to dress the princess in her beautiful new clothes.

Style tips!

Layer different pieces of fabric to create a multi-colored dress.

Place see-through fabric over colored fabric to create pretty layers.

Try using one fabric for the top of the dress and another for the skirt.

You can use any extra fabric or ribbons that you have at home, too.

Style pages

Use these pages to record your favorite outfits and try out new ideas. You could draw the dresses, or stick scraps of pretty paper or material to each page.

Give me a flowery dress.

I want a glitzy outfit!

Make me pretty in pink!

Fill my dress
with patterns.

Dress me
in rainbow
colors.

Design my wedding dress.

Make me a prom dress.

Dress-Up Princess

Activities

Gorgeous gowns

Color the princesses' party dresses.

Draw lines to give each princess a sparkling accessory.

Perfect Princesses

Decorate the tiaras.

Color the princesses' hair.

Prince Charming
Help Prince Charming through the maze to reach the princess.
Start
Finish

Enchanted forest
Draw a beautiful castle.
How many apples
can you count?
....

Princess party
Color the decorations.
Fill the cake stand with delicious treats.

Read the clues, then draw lines to match each princess to her cupcake.

I like sweets.

Pink is my favorite color.

I love chocolate sprinkles.

Draw toppings to finish the cupcakes.

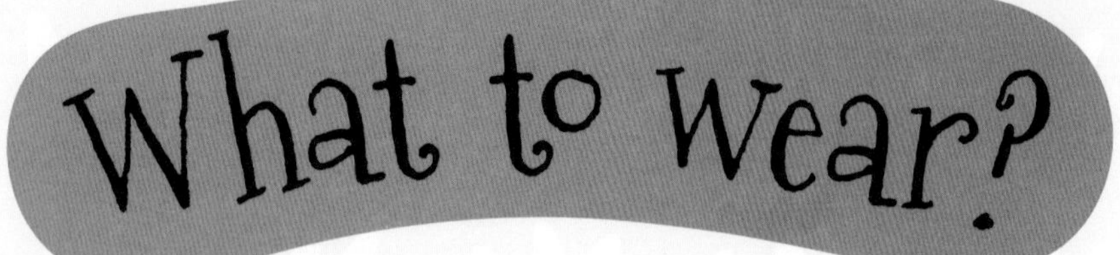

Color the pretty dresses.

Circle your choices.

long	yes/no
sequins	yes/no
sleeves	yes/no
patterned	yes/no
glittery	yes/no

Slipper Search

Circle Cinderella's missing slipper and add color.

The royal ball

Design a beautiful invitation.

Draw lines to give each princess a matching colored crown.

High in the Sky

Decorate the kites.

Follow the strings to see which kite belongs to the princess.

How many kites can you spot?

....

Dream castle

Color the castle and add flags.

Draw princesses in the windows.

Playful Pets
Draw lines to match each princess to her pet.

Pretty as a Picture

Draw a princess in the frame.

Circle five differences between the pictures.

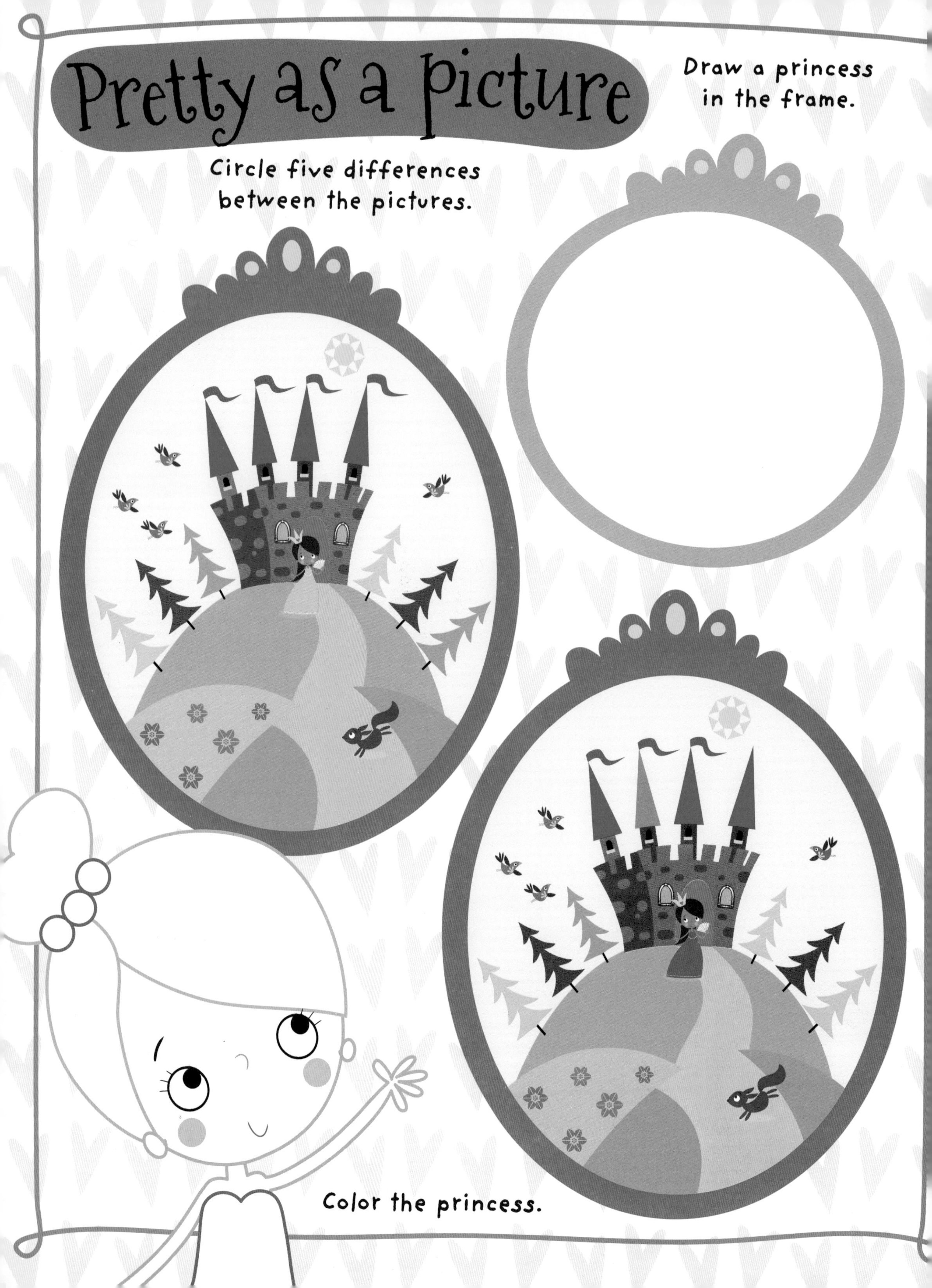

Color the princess.

Royal rides

Color the royal vehicles to make them look glamorous.

Carriage confusion

Follow the lines to see which princess will ride in the carriage.

Color the carriage and horses.

Royal bake-off

The princesses are baking sweet treats!

Decorate the wedding cake.

Circle your choices.

The perfect cupcake

- chocolate yes/no
- frosting yes/no
- sprinkles yes/no
- cherry yes/no

Find the one that doesn't match.

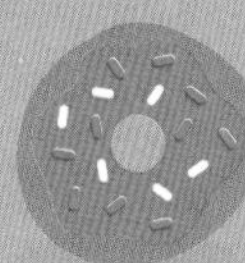

Give the cupcakes a score out of 10.

Castle maze

Help the princesses through the maze to reach the castle.

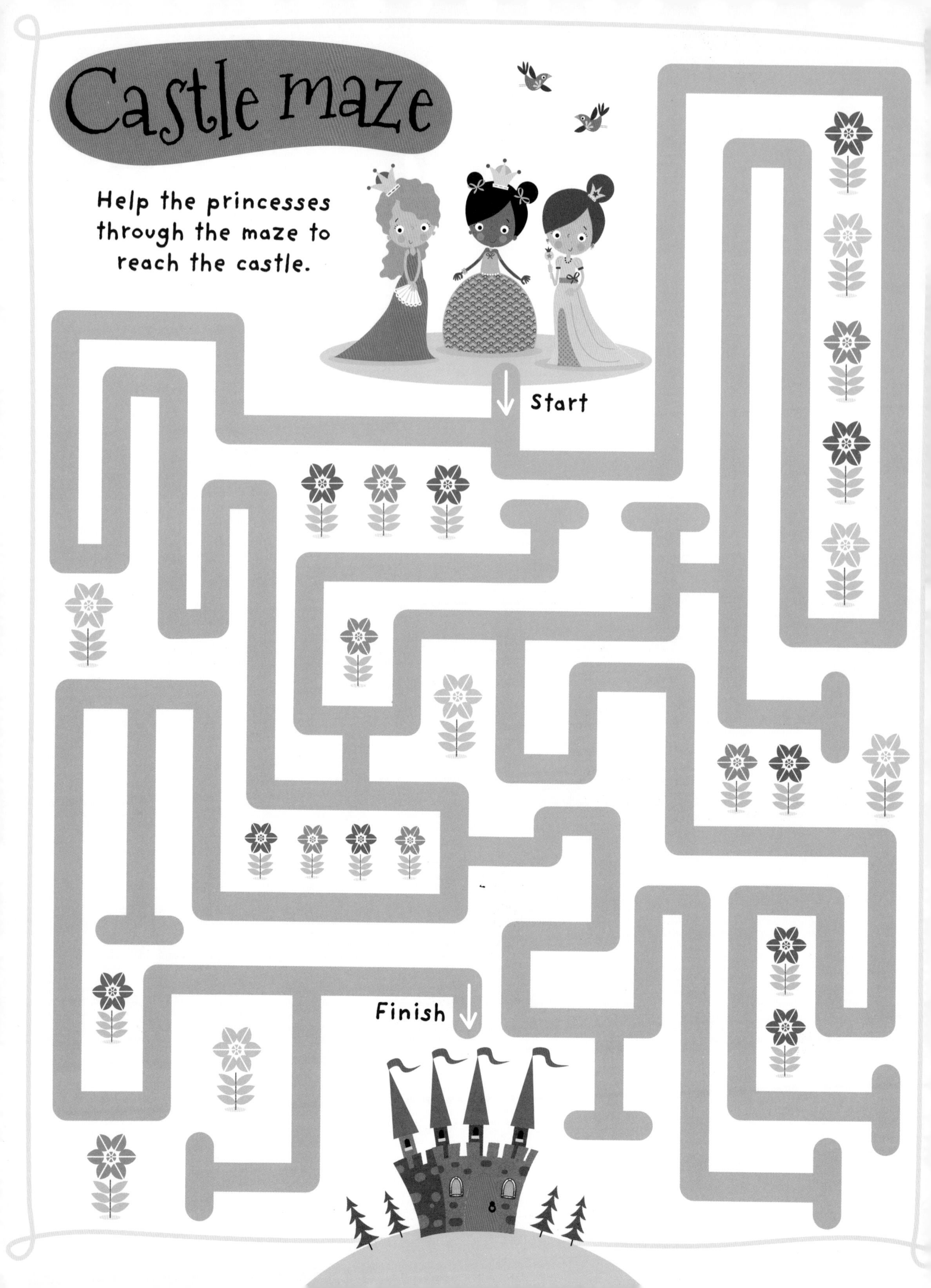

Sparkling jewels
Color the jewels to make them sparkle.
Circle the jewel that doesn't belong.

Pretty Princesses

Circle six differences between the pictures.

Color the princesses' hair.